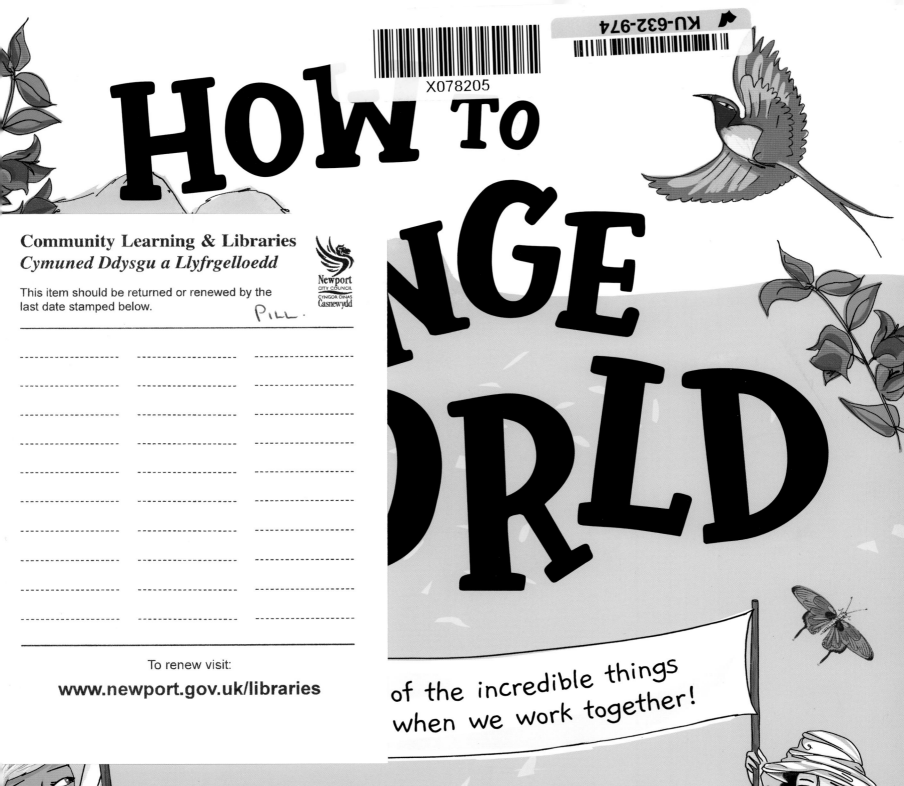

HOW TO ... NGE ORLD

... of the incredible things ... when we work together!

written by
Rashmi Sirdeshpande

illustrated by
Annabel Tempest

PUFFIN

THE FIRST DEMOCRACY

For many years Athens had been a tyranny, which means one person made all the decisions. But in the late sixth century BCE two politicians, Isagoras and Cleisthenes, both wanted to be the leader. Isagoras seized power and soon started acting like a tyrant. But when Isagoras tried to get rid of the boulē (the council of citizens), the people of Athens decided that enough was enough. So they rose up against him.

Isagoras and his supporters fled to the Acropolis, the highest point in the city. The Athenian people trapped them there for two days and nights without any food or water. On the third day, Isagoras and his supporters had to surrender. Cleisthenes, who had been banished, came back to the city to set up a new system – and this time, the *people* would rule Athens.

Demes (tribes) were created across Athens. Members of each deme were randomly chosen to serve on the new boulē and each day one of these people would be randomly chosen to lead it. The boulē decided which matters were to be discussed at the Assembly (a huge gathering of ordinary citizens).

The Assembly met every 9 days and decided everything: even things like whether or not Athens should go to war. Thousands of citizens would turn up. Things that used to be decided by a small group of powerful families were now decided by a vote – a show of hands or a white pebble for yes, a black pebble for no.

To stop tyrants taking over, once a year Athenians had a chance to banish people. Citizens wrote a name on an ostrakon (a piece of broken pottery). If 6,000 people voted, the person whose name came up the most would be banished for 10 years!

Any citizen could speak at the Assembly. From the carpenter and the shoemaker to the merchant and the shipowner – in this system, everyone was equal. Except this didn't actually include everyone! Women, slaves, and people from immigrant families were not considered citizens, so they couldn't vote.

The people of Athens had taken control. At the time, they called this system "isonomia", which means equality. It wasn't perfect. But it was a HUGE change, and the very beginning of what we now call democracy: rule by the people.

The Building of the Great Pyramid

Rising up from the Egyptian desert, on the West Bank of the River Nile, stands the Great Pyramid of Giza. Built over 4,500 years ago, it is an astonishing feat of human engineering. It took thousands of workers 20 years to put together. But how did they manage it?

The pyramid is made up of 2.3 million stone blocks and the smallest ones weigh more than a car! Amazingly, a people that (as far as we know!) hadn't yet discovered wheels, pulleys, or iron tools managed to quarry these blocks, transport them to the construction site, and haul them into place to build a virtually perfect pyramid! It took amazing skill and teamwork.

Ancient Egyptians called it "Ikhet" (glorious light); with its brilliant white stones, the pyramid would have dazzled in the sun. This white limestone came from Tura, 8 miles away; the granite for the inside of the pyramid came from Aswan, 500 miles away; and the copper for tools came from across the Red Sea, in Sinai!

Papyrus rolls tell us that the huge limestone blocks were shipped from Tura to Giza and taken through manmade canals right to the foot of the pyramid. Egyptologists think the workers then used giant sledges to pull the blocks to the pyramid. But this still doesn't explain how they managed to lift the blocks into place! There are lots of theories about ramps but we don't know how they worked. Did they zigzag up one side? Curve around the whole thing? Build it from the inside? It's a mystery.

The Great Pyramid was built for King Khufu. Two slightly smaller pyramids were later built for Khufu's son Khafre and his grandson Menkaure on the same site.

The Great Pyramid is also amazingly precise. The outer stones are cut to sit together so tightly that you can't even fit a knife's blade between them. The pyramid even points to true north – Ancient Egyptians followed the positions of two stars to get this right. It's impressive even by today's building standards, but it's a marvel for the Bronze Age! The workers were highly skilled craftsmen (not slaves, as it was once thought), and they worked together like a well-oiled machine.

To lay all these blocks in 20 years, they'd have had to place 1 block every 2 minutes during sunlight hours!

The Great Pyramid was 480 feet tall — that's the height of over 30 London buses!

Ancient Egyptian art and hieroglyphics teach us so much about how people lived but they say nothing about how the Great Pyramid was built. That's probably no accident. It wasn't designed to be understood – it was designed to be WONDERED at. However it was built, it is an amazing example of what humans can do when they use their talents and work together.

The Matchwomen's Strike

Working-class women were looked down upon in Victorian England – especially the matchwomen from London's East End. However, on 2 July 1888, 1,400 of them walked out of the Bryant & May factory in protest against their terrible working conditions – and they surprised everyone with their strength and determination.

NEVER MIND YOUR FINGERS!

At the time, the matchwomen were working 14 hours a day for very little pay. They were fined for tiny things like talking or taking a toilet break. They worked with dangerous machinery, and the foremen who ran the factory floor didn't care if they got hurt.

They even had to work with a nasty substance called white phosphorous, which could lead to a painful, life-threatening illness they called "phossy jaw". If they complained, they were sacked!

When Annie Besant (a campaigner) heard about this, she secretly interviewed some of the matchwomen. Then she wrote a shocking article in a newspaper called *The Link*.

Bryant & May were furious. They tried to bully the matchwomen into saying that the article was full of lies. When the matchwomen refused, one worker was sacked, and that was it: 1,400 matchwomen went on strike. They quickly blocked the factory door, held large meetings, and made a committee to put forward their demands. Historians used to think that Annie had organized the strike but we now know this isn't true – the matchwomen did everything themselves! Bryant & May had underestimated them.

Times were tough and the strikers were penniless, but they stuck together and looked after one another.

TROUBLEMAKERS:
Alice Francis
Kate Slater
Mary Driscoll
Jane Wakeling
Eliza Martin

NO MORE PHOSSY JAW BRYANT & MAY

They did it! They really did it!

They stick together, those girls . . .

Everyone in the city was talking about the strike. The newspapers even raised money to help. The matchwomen raised money too, singing in the streets and talking to anyone who would listen.

On 11 July, 56 matchwomen marched into parliament. Traffic stopped. People laughed at them, but they marched on and stunned the politicians with their intelligence and directness.

By 18 July, there was so much pressure on Bryant & May that they gave in to all the matchwomen's demands. The fines were cancelled, working conditions were improved, and the women were able to set up the Union of Women Match Makers. This was a big win and a huge inspiration for the Great Dock Strike of 1889, which took place just down the road. ("Remember the matchgirls!" leader John Burns told the dockers.) They had won their battle and set an example for many other workers.

THE CAMPAIGN FOR VOTES FOR WOMEN

For centuries, women all over the world have been fighting for the right to vote – to have a say in how their countries are run. They have organized public meetings and marches, and gathered signatures, all demanding the vote. And, in many cases, they have won.

We obey laws so we want a say in how they're made!

Votes for women didn't always mean ALL women. Australia and Canada gave women the vote in 1902 and 1918 but the indigenous women and men of these countries couldn't vote until the 1960s. In South Africa, white women were given the right to vote from 1930 but black women had to wait until 1993. And, in Britain, only some women got the vote in 1918 – it wasn't until 1928 that all women had the same voting rights as men.

We pay taxes so we want a say in how that money is spent!

Not all protests were peaceful. In the 1900s, a British group called the Suffragettes smashed windows and set fire to postboxes to draw attention to their cause. They were arrested many times, but they never gave up! Working-class women played a big role, risking their jobs to join the campaign.

1893 — New Zealand was the first country to give women the vote.

I can't believe I am still protesting this stuff

Russian women won the right to vote in 1917 after 40,000 women marched through St Petersburg, led by female guards on white horses.

In Switzerland, women couldn't vote until 1971. They had been campaigning since the 1880s but the law could only be changed by a vote. Only men could vote and they kept saying no. In 1928, after British women got the vote, Swiss activists marched a giant model snail through the streets of Bern to show their anger at how S L O W their country was being!

The right to vote has now been won in many countries, but women can't always use that right. And in some places it's not safe for them to vote. Big changes like this take time to be accepted. But winning the right to vote is an important first step.

WOMEN of the WORLD UNITE

THE MONTGOMERY BUS BOYCOTT

In the 1950s, the American South had strict segregation laws, which meant that black people had to sit in separate sections of public buses. If the white section was full, black people were expected to give up their seats.

On 1 December 1955, when Rosa Parks refused to give up her seat on a Montgomery bus, she was arrested. She wasn't the first black woman to refuse or to be arrested for refusing, but this time it was different. Rosa was well respected in the black community. Her simple act triggered a bus boycott that lasted 381 days and marked the start of the US civil rights movement.

NO BUS

BUS BOYCOTT

DON'T RIDE THE BUS!

"Do not ride the buses to work, to town, to school, or anywhere, on Monday."

On the night of her arrest, a group of teachers printed 52,000 leaflets calling for a bus boycott on 5 December, the day of Rosa's trial. They secretly distributed them in black schools, churches, and neighbourhoods.

It worked. Despite the risk to their jobs and safety, over 90% of the black community stayed off the buses on that cold morning.

When Rosa was found guilty, a campaign group led by pastor Martin Luther King Jr voted to extend the boycott. Black taxi drivers helped by reducing their fares to match bus fares (until the city banned them!). Thousands walked to school and work. A carpool system was started but the police bullied the drivers with fines and warnings. Meanwhile, with hardly any passengers, the Montgomery bus company was struggling.

In January, King's house was bombed but he urged everyone to stay calm – this had to be a peaceful protest. In February, the city called for the arrest of over 80 boycott leaders, including King. They turned themselves in. King's trial was first and though he was found guilty and fined $500, he walked out of the courtroom to cheering crowds.

On 13 November 1956, the city banned carpools. But that same day, King got some news that changed everything: the US Supreme Court had ruled that bus segregation was unconstitutional! The order took 5 weeks to reach Montgomery where people were still boycotting. They had been walking for over a year.

My feets is tired but my soul is rested!

On 21 December 1956, King and his colleagues quietly took a front-row seat on Montgomery's first desegregated bus. The boycott had worked. There was still a long road ahead, but this was a start to ending segregation.

The Fight to Save the Whales

Humans have hunted whales for thousands of years. Whales used to be killed with hand-thrown harpoons, and hunting was limited to the coastlines, so there were still lots of whales in the ocean.

But over time, boats became bigger and faster, hunting equipment became deadlier and whaling expanded into the open oceans. By the eighteenth century, whaling had become a big business: whale oil was used in everything from cars and trains to soap and lamps. In the 1950s alone, almost half a million whales were killed – and that's just in the Southern Hemisphere! By the 1970s, some species like the humpback whale and the blue whale were at risk of extinction.

In 1970, biologist Roger Payne recorded the beautiful and complex songs of the humpback whales. The songs changed the way people thought about whales. Activist groups began to use them in their global campaigns.

Some groups, such as Greenpeace, set out on dangerous voyages to stop whaleships on the hunt. They took photos and video footage and shared them with the world for the first time ever. They even put their own bodies between the whales and the whalers' harpoons.

Lots of groups were working together to save the whales. And, over time, this made a real difference: public pressure was so strong that in 1982 the International Whaling Commission (the IWC) announced a global ban on commercial whaling, which started in 1986. It wasn't a total ban, though – it was a quota system to stop countries overhunting. This gave whale populations some time to recover.

Nowadays, a few thousand whales are still killed each year, but there has been a big reduction since the ban. Many species of whale have made a promising recovery, especially the humpback whale.

Blue whales can weigh up to 200 tons – that's twice the weight of the largest dinosaur! Or as much as 33 elephants!

Sadly, the ban is under threat and whaling is increasing again. Iceland, Japan and Norway are still hunting whales. And in December 2018, Japan announced that it was leaving the IWC and restarting commercial whaling.

Whales are also under threat from pollution, global warming, collisions with ships, and getting entangled in abandoned fishing nets. Campaigns and international organizations have done a LOT to bring whales back from the brink of extinction. But their future isn't certain, and these incredible creatures still need protecting.

The Start of Fairer Trade

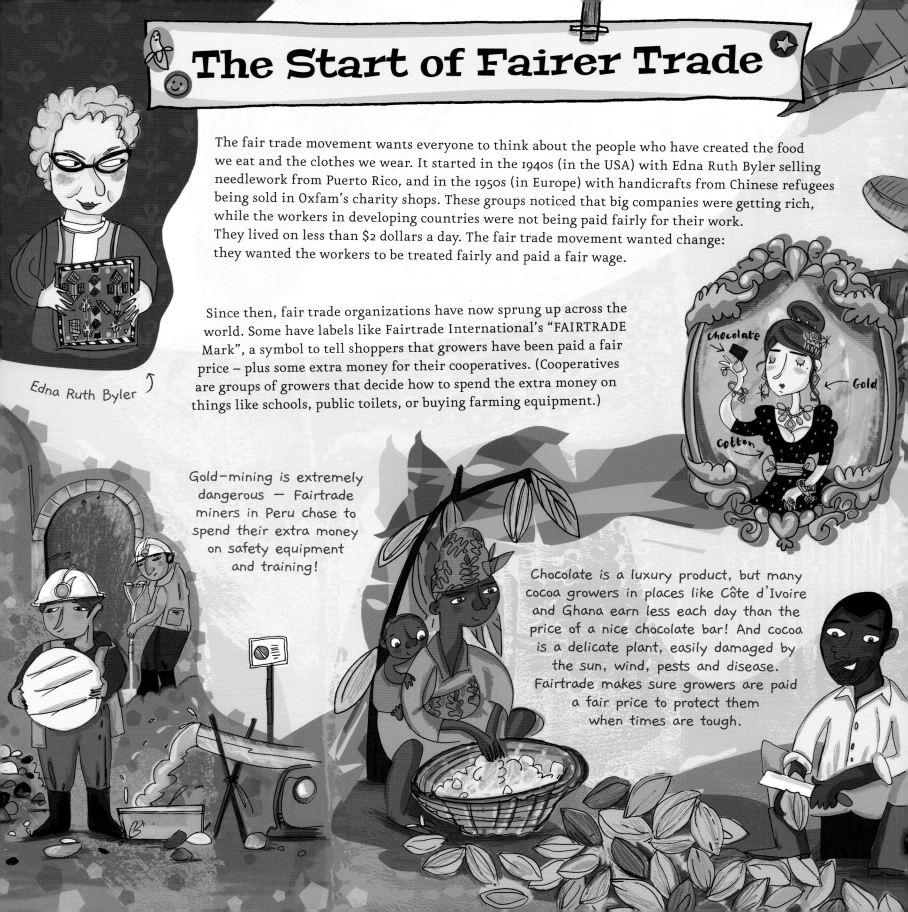

The fair trade movement wants everyone to think about the people who have created the food we eat and the clothes we wear. It started in the 1940s (in the USA) with Edna Ruth Byler selling needlework from Puerto Rico, and in the 1950s (in Europe) with handicrafts from Chinese refugees being sold in Oxfam's charity shops. These groups noticed that big companies were getting rich, while the workers in developing countries were not being paid fairly for their work. They lived on less than $2 dollars a day. The fair trade movement wanted change: they wanted the workers to be treated fairly and paid a fair wage.

Since then, fair trade organizations have now sprung up across the world. Some have labels like Fairtrade International's "FAIRTRADE Mark", a symbol to tell shoppers that growers have been paid a fair price – plus some extra money for their cooperatives. (Cooperatives are groups of growers that decide how to spend the extra money on things like schools, public toilets, or buying farming equipment.)

Edna Ruth Byler ↱

chocolate

Gold

cotton

Gold-mining is extremely dangerous — Fairtrade miners in Peru chose to spend their extra money on safety equipment and training!

Chocolate is a luxury product, but many cocoa growers in places like Côte d'Ivoire and Ghana earn less each day than the price of a nice chocolate bar! And cocoa is a delicate plant, easily damaged by the sun, wind, pests and disease. Fairtrade makes sure growers are paid a fair price to protect them when times are tough.

Ordinary people have helped spread the word, buying fair trade and encouraging others to do the same. Today, all sorts of things are fair trade: coffee, chocolate, sugar, fruits, rice, flowers, cotton, and even gold.

Over half the bananas sold in Switzerland are now Fairtrade bananas!

It's not a perfect system. It doesn't help the growers who aren't part of cooperatives, and it doesn't always consider other issues (like the environment).

HAPPY BANANAS

FAIR TRADE

Despite the challenges, the FAIRTRADE Mark is still trusted around the world and it continues to make a difference to hundreds of thousands of growers and their families. It's a step in the right direction: the movement has encouraged everyone to remember that there are people behind the things we buy, and what it means to be fair to them.

The Healing of the Ozone Layer

The ozone layer is a layer of gas in the atmosphere that acts like sunscreen for Planet Earth, shielding it from ultraviolet (UV) rays from the sun. These harmful rays can cause skin cancer and eye problems in humans, and can affect plants and animals too. In the 1970s, scientists discovered that the ozone layer had become dangerously thin in places. This was because of chemicals called CFCs (chlorofluorocarbons), which were used in things like refrigerators, foam packaging, and aerosol sprays.

The scientists tried to convince governments to ban CFCs – but the big industries that used CFCs insisted that there wasn't enough evidence. It can't be true, they said. But more and more scientific reports started coming out to say that the ozone layer was in trouble. Then, in the mid-1980s, US space agency NASA confirmed that the scientists were right. The ozone layer had been severely damaged. Something had to be done to protect the planet, and fast.

CFCs

In 1987, a group of countries got together to sign the Montreal Protocol, an agreement to gradually ban CFCs. 193 countries had signed it by 1989 and by 2009 all 197 United Nations countries had signed – this was the first time they had all agreed on a course of action. While CFCs were being phased out, ordinary people helped by boycotting products like hairsprays. Everyone knew about CFCs, and anyone could make a difference – even schoolchildren.

ARRRrghh!

← CFCs

ozone

Atoms are the building blocks of the universe. Ozone is made up of 3 oxygen atoms joined together (we call this an ozone molecule). CFC molecules contain chlorine, and when the sun's UV rays hit them, they break them up. These freed chlorine atoms break up ozone molecules much faster than new ozone can be made. This is how, over time, the ozone layer was damaged.

Thanks to the CFC ban, it now looks like the ozone layer is repairing itself. Scientists say that the thinnest parts (over the North and South Poles) should be completely healed by the 2060s. There is *much* more we can do to protect our planet, but the success of the Montreal Protocol shows that when countries work together and people make choices that are better for our planet, it is possible for the Earth to heal.

THE FIGHT AGAINST POLIO

Polio is a potentially deadly disease that mostly affects children under 5 years old. It can also cause paralysis and there's no cure – but it is preventable. In 1988, there were 350,000 cases across 125 countries. But, thanks to an ENORMOUS global campaign involving 20 MILLION volunteers, by 2018 there were only 33 cases and they were found only in two countries: Afghanistan and Pakistan.

In 1985, Rotary, a charity set up by ordinary people, decided they wanted to eradicate polio – from the entire world! It was such a big goal that, at first, even the World Health Organization didn't think it could be done. Humans have only ever eradicated one disease: smallpox. This would be a massive project: vaccines had to be cheap, easy to use, kept cool, and – because of how polio is spread – they had to reach every single child in the world!

Rotary first ran immunization projects in the Philippines and in Central and South America. This made the world health community sit up and listen. Perhaps eradication *was* possible? In 1988, a global alliance was formed, and slowly, other supporters came on board too.

India had the biggest share of polio cases: with its fast-growing population and tropical climate, the disease spread quickly. But with the help of detailed plans and satellite technology to locate children – and an army of local volunteers to reach them – it WAS wiped out. Volunteers went door to door and set up booths at bus stops and train stations to catch people on the move.

Volunteers across the world have used boats, motorbikes, helicopters, and even camels to reach children! They've navigated conflict zones in Afghanistan and worked with the military in Pakistan for access and information. It hasn't been easy, but the campaign has always kept its eye on its goal: to vaccinate every single child.

The war in Afghanistan and the difficulty of finding moving populations in Pakistan mean that delivering the last vaccines will be very difficult. But we are SO close to eradicating polio. And if humans can do this, maybe we could one day eradicate other diseases too . . .

Goodbye Polio!

The International Space Station

Flying through space, 240 miles above the Earth, the ISS is a giant space lab. It lets us learn how humans can adapt to living in space – which is very important for future space exploration. The ISS is a HUGE project by 5 different space agencies from around the world: NASA (from the USA), Roscosmos (from Russia), the Canadian Space Agency, JAXA (from Japan), and the European Space Agency. A project like this is ONLY possible if countries work together.

The ISS was assembled in space, piece by piece, with each space agency providing a different section. It couldn't be put together on the ground – there's no rocket powerful enough to launch a space station that's as big as a football pitch! The ISS is so big that it took over 12 years to assemble. And this all had to be done while it was flying at 17,000 miles per hour, making a lap of the Earth every 90 minutes.

The ISS is fully solar-powered and it's so bright that you might spot it as it flies over your country. It's the third-brightest thing in the sky after the sun and moon and it looks like a super-fast plane. You can see where it is right now using NASA's Spot the Station website.

Astronauts and cosmonauts have to exercise for 2 hours a day so they don't lose bone and muscle mass (because they're not used enough in space).

There are small robots on the ISS — they help with things like repairs and taking pictures. Some can even chat and play music!

All kinds of experiments are conducted on the ISS — like growing vegetables in space.

A special space system on the ISS recycles urine into drinking water.

This robotic arm (Canadarm2) helps with construction and repair work. It also grabs on to space vehicles to help them land on the station and deliver people, equipment, and supplies.

Spacewalks to do experiments or repair the ISS are very dangerous. Astronauts/cosmonauts work in pairs, tethered to the station so they don't float away. Spacesuits help them breathe and protect them from extreme temperatures.

Now, space agencies have set their sights on building the "Gateway", a station in the moon's orbit. This would be a launchpad for exploring the moon, Mars, and beyond. But space exploration is expensive and complex – it's too big a challenge for any one country. If we are going to do this, we will have to do it together … .

The Singing Revolution

Music has always had a special place in the hearts of Estonians. It is their way of holding on to their language, their stories, and their hope.

A small country in Eastern Europe, Estonia has been ruled by other countries for most of the last 800 years. By the 1980s, it had been occupied by the Soviet Union for 40 years, because of a secret pact between the Soviet Union and Nazi Germany. The Estonians said this pact was illegal and that Estonia had always been a free nation – and they used their songs to tell this to the world.

One of the ways they did this was through the Song Festival (Laulupidu), an Estonian tradition that goes back to 1869. Usually held at the Song Festival Grounds in the capital, Tallinn, the Song Festivals were huge – up to 30,000 people on stage and over 100,000 in the audience! In the Soviet years, Estonians were forced to sing about Communist leaders like Marx and Lenin. But, in 1947, they sneaked in a patriotic poem that became Estonia's unofficial national anthem. It was then sung at the end of every song festival. The Soviets once tried to ban it but the crowd started singing it and would not stop.

In June 1988, people gathered in the Song Festival Grounds for 6 nights straight, singing, swaying, and waving banned Estonian flags!

Singing united the people. Meanwhile, activists were getting bolder, making speeches about independence. In August 1989, on the 50th anniversary of the Nazi–Soviet pact, around 2 million Estonians, Latvians, and Lithuanians held hands to make a human chain over 400 miles long from Tallinn (in Estonia) to Vilnius (in Lithuania). They peacefully protested against Soviet occupation.

One day, no matter what, we will win!

Things came to a head in August 1991 when Communist extremists in Moscow tried to take over. They sent tanks into Estonia and even tried to take over the TV tower and radio stations, but unarmed Estonians protected them. After a long wait, there was news that the takeover attempt in Moscow had failed. Soviet troops withdrew from Estonia and, that night, Estonia's political leaders declared Estonia an independent republic. In 1994, Estonians held their first Laulupidu as a nation free from Soviet rule – and they sang with all their hearts.

The End of Slavery in the British Empire

The British abolitionists believed that slavery was wrong because humans should never be owned by others and bought and sold like objects.

Slavery had existed for thousands of years and, by the 1700s, hundreds of thousands of Africans were being crammed into British slave ships bound for the Americas. The slaves who survived the journey were forced to work, often on sugar plantations in the Caribbean. There, they were treated terribly, working long hours in the burning sun. But then, in the 1780s, the British abolition movement began, with one clear goal: to put an end to the slave trade.

Abolition of SLAVERY

Sugar was a huge business and the people making money from it (including politicians!) didn't want the slave trade to end. But the abolitionists didn't give up. They published anti-slavery pamphlets. They brought hundreds of petitions to parliament with signatures from people across the country, rich and poor.

The campaign opened people's eyes to the suffering of slaves. Freed slaves like Olaudah Equiano published their life-stories. Slave-ship captains and crew talked about the horrible conditions on the ships. Many people couldn't read so the abolitionists shared the shocking image of a slave ship with 454 Africans shackled below the decks.

Let justice be done!

THE INTERESTING NARRATIVE of the life of OLAUDAH EQUIANO

I'm not having slave-grown sugar in MY cup of tea!

Poets and writers wrote about slavery, and people refused to buy slave-grown sugar. Over 300,000 people joined in.

Meanwhile, slaves were bravely rebelling on plantations everywhere, even though they were punished severely. In the 1790s, thousands of slaves rose up in the French colony of Haiti and eventually declared the country independent in 1804. This inspired revolts across the Caribbean.

The news scared British slave-owners, who wondered whether slavery was cursed. The abolitionists persisted with their campaign and in 1807 the slave trade was abolished.

Britain would no longer ship new slaves from Africa. So, the abolitionists then set another goal: to free existing slaves. It took another 30 years, but by 1838 all slaves in the British Empire had been freed. Slavery was illegal in Britain and throughout the British Empire.

In all, over 10 million Africans had been shipped to the Americas as slaves, a third of them on British ships. That's the same number of people who live in Sweden today!

Sadly, slavery still exists in the world. But the abolitionist campaign shows that when we persevere and work together, change is possible.

The 1965 Freedom Ride

The indigenous people of Australia (the Aboriginal and Torres Strait Islander people) have lived in Australia for over 50,000 years. But when British explorer James Cook arrived by ship in 1788, he declared the country *terra nullius* – "no one's land". Over the next 200 years, as European settlers moved in, indigenous people were treated appallingly. They were forced out of their homes and moved to missions, reserves, and stations. They were kept separate from non-indigenous people and weren't even counted as part of the Australian population.

But the world was changing. Just like the black civil rights movement in the United States, a movement was growing in Australia too.

In 1965, around 30 Sydney University students went on the Freedom Ride – a 2-week bus ride through New South Wales to show just how bad things were for indigenous people and to encourage them to speak out against discrimination. The Freedom Riders protested in places where indigenous people were banned. They took records and made films to show the poor living conditions of indigenous people, how they weren't allowed in the same shops or clubs, and how they had to sit at the front in cinemas (if they were allowed in at all).

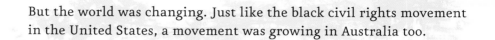

The students were led by Charlie Perkins, one of the first indigenous Australians to go to university.

The Freedom Riders met with a lot of resistance from local non-indigenous people who were angry about the protests. At one point in their journey, the Freedom Riders' bus was followed by a car and run off the road and into a ditch! And when the students took a group of indigenous children for a swim at the Moree swimming pool (where they were banned), a crowd of non-indigenous people turned up, shouting and booing at them and throwing eggs.

The Freedom Ride was all over the news. The Freedom Riders' protests and the resistance they faced opened the eyes of many Australians – when they saw what was happening in their own country, they were shocked. Discrimination wasn't just a problem in places like the United States and South Africa – it was happening in their backyard and it was not acceptable.

Two years later, in the 1967 referendum, 90% of Australians voted to have indigenous people counted as part of the population and for the Australian government to make laws to help their communities. There is still much work to be done, but this was an important step in a long campaign for equality.

THE TREEPLANTERS OF PIPLANTRI

The village of Piplantri is a green oasis in the dry and dusty Rajsamand district of Rajasthan, India. But it hasn't always been this way. By the early 2000s, marble mining had destroyed much of the land. Farmers struggled to grow crops, and many had to leave to find work in nearby cities, leaving their families behind. Even Piplantri's local wildlife had begun to disappear.

Then, in 2007, village chief Sunder Paliwal made an important decision. Heartbroken after his daughter's death, he decided that, whenever a girl was born in the village, 111 trees would be planted in her honour.

Not only that – parents would promise to send their daughter to school and that they wouldn't let her be married before she turned 18 (child marriages are a big problem in Rajasthan). And the villagers and the parents would pay for the girl's education, together.

For me, everything is linked: the girl child, the land, water, animals, birds, trees.

This project made a HUGE difference. Piplantri's villagers used to be upset when a girl was born because daughters eventually leave home to live with their husband's families (while sons stay and earn money for their parents and look after them when they are old). Girls are considered expensive too – traditional Indian families expect the girl's family to pay for the wedding. But thanks to Piplantri's new project, the birth of a girl wouldn't be something to worry about – it would be something to celebrate.

Now, the villagers plant trees for all their major life events. So far, they've planted over a quarter of a million – all kinds of trees from mango and neem trees to Indian rosewood. They've also planted lots of aloe vera plants, which protect the trees from insects and give local women a way of earning money (they sell aloe vera gel, juice and pickle). The villagers have even worked together to build dams to raise the dangerously low water levels, helping keep the forest rich and green.

The tree project has changed everything for Piplantri. Birds and animals that had disappeared have started to return. Some of the villagers who had left for the city have moved back home. And all of Piplantri's girls now go to school. In a world where girls are too often valued less than boys, these girls are celebrated.

THE FIGHT FOR MARRIAGE EQUALITY

People have not always been allowed to marry whoever they want.
Sadly, in some countries, they still aren't. For many, many years, across the world,
only a man and woman have been allowed to get married.
But not all families look like that.

Some look like this . . .

. . . Or this.

And every family is different!

The marriage equality movement is a campaign about LOVE.
It believes that people should be free to love whoever they love.
This campaign has been supported by many people: from politicians
and celebrities to hundreds of thousands of ordinary people.

Some people have protested in courts for the right to marry. Others have marched
through the streets. In 2001, the Netherlands became the first country to make
same-sex marriage legal. Belgium, Canada, Spain, and South Africa followed.
But some countries took a lot longer, like Brazil (2013), the UK (2014),
the US (2015), and Australia (2017).

In February 2004, same-sex couples in San Francisco in the United States protested by getting married! For one whole month, the mayor ignored state laws and gave marriage licences to over 4,000 same-sex couples. When the California Supreme Court declared these marriages illegal, people protested in the streets. There was a long legal battle and same-sex marriage was finally allowed in California in 2013. Eventually, in 2015, the United States Supreme Court ordered all states to allow same-sex marriages.

The rainbow flag is sometimes used in the marriage equality movement to show pride, hope, and togetherness.

Love wins!

love

RIGHTS FOR ALL

BEING GAY ISN'T A CHOICE. HATE IS.

IT'S JUST LOVE

In some countries, the people have to vote to change the law. The Irish people voted on same-sex marriage in 2015 and their answer was an overwhelming YES. The people of Australia were asked the same question in 2017 and they had the same answer: YES.

LOVE

The marriage equality movement has meant that many same-sex couples can now get married. But there are still many countries where only a man and woman can marry. And all over the world some people are still treated badly because of who they love. There is so much more to do, but the marriage equality movement has made a huge difference to many lives.

For YOU, the reader, and all the amazing things you'll do – R.S.

For my boys, Finbar, Dougal and Rufus – go change the world brilliantly! – A.T.

PUFFIN BOOKS

UK | USA | Canada | Ireland | Australia | India | New Zealand | South Africa

Puffin Books is part of the Penguin Random House group of companies whose
addresses can be found at global.penguinrandomhouse.com.

www.penguin.co.uk   www.puffin.co.uk   www.ladybird.co.uk

Penguin
Random House
UK

First published 2020

001

Printed in China

A CIP catalogue record for this book is available from the British Library

ISBN: 978–0–241–41034–9

All correspondence to:
Puffin Books, Penguin Random House Children's
One Embassy Gardens, New Union Square
5 Nine Elms Lane, London SW8 5DA